This book belongs to:

....

....

A NEW BURLINGTON BOOK

Editor: Ruth Symons
Designer: Bianca Lucas

This edition first published in 2018 by QED Publishing,
an imprint of The Quarto Group.
The Old Brewery, 6 Blundell Street
London N7 9BH, United Kingdom.
T (0)20 7700 6700 F (0)20 7700 8066
www.QuartoKnows.com

A catalogue record for this book is available from
the British Library.

ISBN 978 1 78171 360 0

Manufactured in Guangdong, China TT042018

1 2 3 4 5 6 7 8 9

The Not-So-Perfect Penguin

Penguin

Steve Smallman

NEW BURLINGTON

On a snowy, blowy island in the middle of the sea lived a group of perfect penguins. They were **smart** and **serious** and **sensible**.

All except for Percy, who was...

well...

not so perfect.

The other penguins ate their dinner sensibly.
But Percy always played with his food.

"Eat nicely, Percy!"
the biggest penguin said.

While the other penguins **waddled** along seriously, Percy **slid** on his tummy.

"Be careful, Percy," the oldest penguin grumbled.

The other penguins swam smoothly through the water, catching lots of fish. But Percy liked to jump and play, turning somersaults and landing with a big...

SPLASH!

"Look out, Percy," the smallest penguin said. "You silly penguin!"

When it was really cold, all the
penguins huddled together.
Percy felt **warm** and **safe**
in the middle of the group.

But then, **oh dear**, he needed to...

"Ew, Percy," the penguins said.
"You smelly penguin!"

They went and stood away from Percy.

Percy waddled away sadly.
"My friends think I'm **silly** and **smelly**.
I'll never be **perfect** like them..."

The snow fell harder and the wind blew stronger.
"It's cold on my own," said Percy, shivering.

Percy made himself a new friend from snow and ice,
but the snow penguin wasn't very warm to cuddle up to.

Without Percy, the penguins ate their dinner sensibly.

"It's so quiet!" the oldest penguin said.

They swam seriously, without splashing.

"It's rather dull!" the biggest penguin said.

They waddled along
in a smart line.

"It's a bit boring!"
the fluffiest penguin said.

"I wish Percy
was here," the
smallest penguin said.

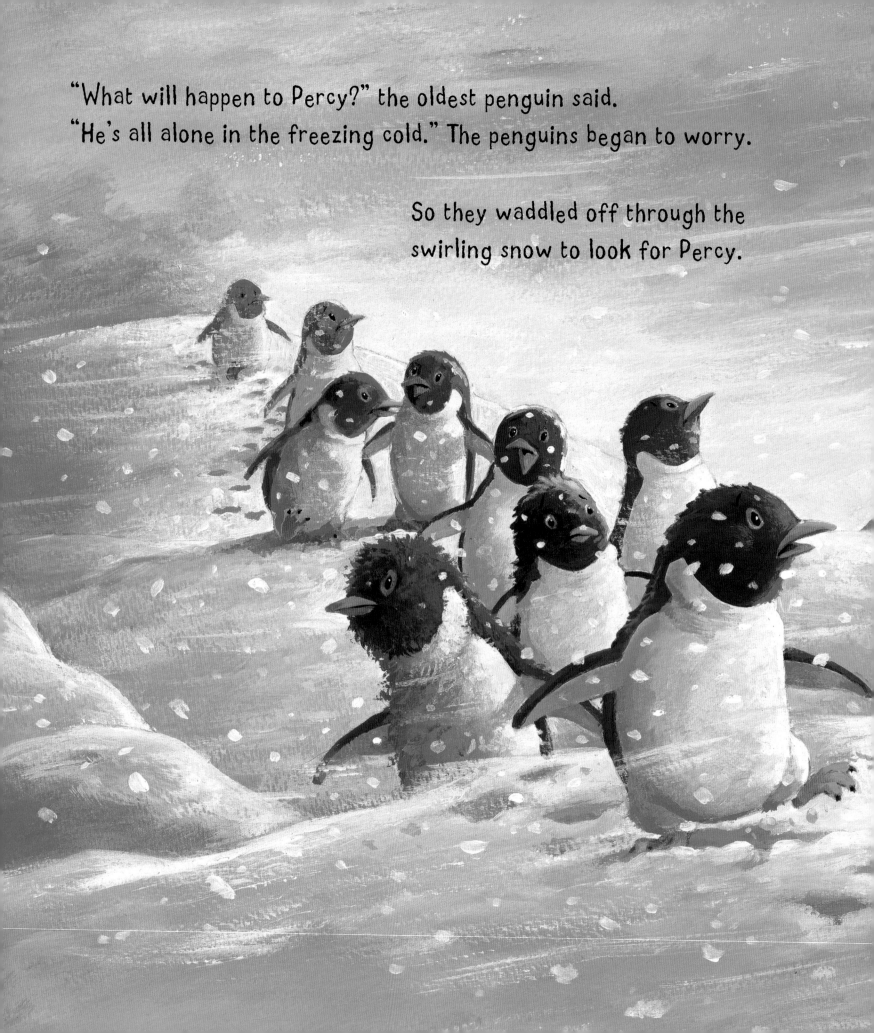

"What will happen to Percy?" the oldest penguin said.
"He's all alone in the freezing cold." The penguins began to worry.

So they waddled off through the
swirling snow to look for Percy.

In an icy cave, they found two snow penguins.
One had lost its beak, but the other looked familiar.

It was Percy!

All the penguins gathered around and cuddled him.
Slowly, slowly, the snow began to melt.

Drip... drip... drip.

When Percy's flippers were free of snow,
he stretched and then...

TICKLE...

TICKLE...

TICKLE!

The penguins all fell about laughing.

"Oh Percy," the smallest penguin giggled.
"It's good to have you back!"

Surrounded by happy penguins, Percy felt that
maybe he didn't need to be perfect after all.
His friends loved him just as he was.

NEXT STEPS

Show the children the cover again. Could they have guessed what the story is about just from looking at the cover?

Percy is playful, but some of his actions annoy the other penguins. Ask the children if they think Percy was annoying or if he was just having fun. Have the children ever annoyed somebody when they were playing?

Penguins live together in big groups called colonies. Many types of penguin live in the cold, icy regions of Antarctica. They huddle together to keep warm in the coldest winter months. Do the children think it was mean of the penguins to leave Percy out of the huddle? Have they ever ignored a friend who annoyed them?

Percy thinks he doesn't fit in because he's not perfect like the other penguins. Do the children ever feel like they don't fit in? Discuss what this feels like. Explain to the children that we're all slightly different but we're all good at something.

Were the other penguins happier after Percy had gone? Ask the children why they think the penguins decided to go and find him.

Ask the children which penguin is their favourite. Is it Percy? Or maybe it's the fluffiest penguin or the oldest penguin. How many times can they spot their favourite penguin?